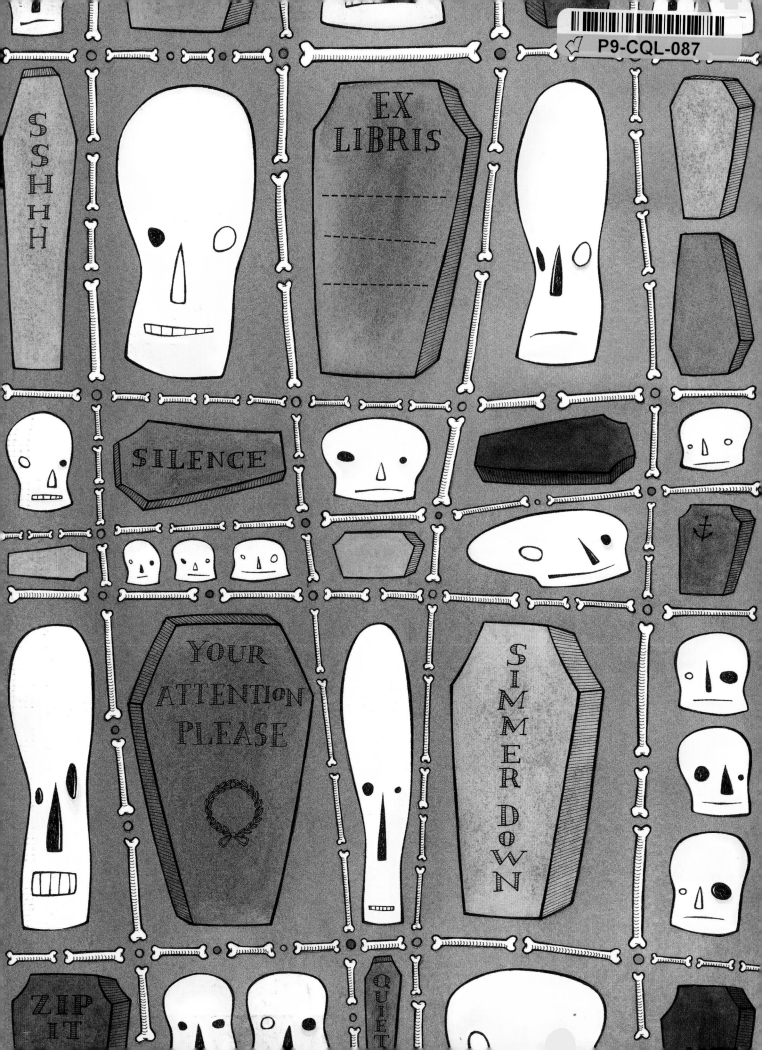

For Doug, Angela, and Meaghan —M. A. H.
For my nephew Sam —S. E. K.

Special thanks to Michael Rex
for loaning his idea for "Goodnight, Goon."

Text copyright © 2004 by Monica A. Harris
Illustrations and hand lettering copyright © 2004 by Susan Estelle Kwas

First published in the United States of America in 2004 by
Walker Publishing Company, Inc.

Published simultaneously in Canada by Fitzhenry and Whiteside, Markham, Ontario L3R 4T8

For information about permission to reproduce selections from
this book, write to Permissions, Walker & Company,
104 Fifth Avenue, New York, New York 10011.

The artist used ink and watercolor on 140-lb. cold-press
Winsor & Newton paper to create the illustrations for this book.

Book design by Victoria Allen & Marlene Tungseth

Visit Walker & Company's Web site at www.walkeryoungreaders.com

Library of Congress Cataloging-in-Publication Data

Harris, Monica, 1964-
Wake the dead / Monica A. Harris ; illustrations by Susan Estelle Kwas.
p. cm.
Summary: Although he has been warned that he will wake the dead, Henry continues to make too much noise
until the warning comes true, and then he must find a way to help the dead rest in peace again.
ISBN 0-8027-8922-6 (HC) — ISBN 0-8027-8923-4 (RE)
[1. Noise—Fiction. 2. Zombies—Fiction.] I. Kwas, Susan Estelle, ill. II. Title.

PZ7.H2433Wak 2004
[Fic]—dc22
2003070535

Printed in Hong Kong
2 4 6 8 10 9 7 5 3 1

Henry was having a loud day. When he played, it was loud. When he walked, it was loud. When he talked, it was loud. Everything he did was loud.

POW!
SPLAT! KerPLOP!

"Hush up, son," Henry's father said,
"or you'll wake the dead."

And wouldn't you know it . . . .

he did!

The dead rose from their graves. They emerged from their coffins. They pushed open their mausoleum doors.

WHAT WAS ALL THIS NOISE?! No bones about it, this just wouldn't do! They had been dead to the world, but now they were awake and grumpy. With a yawn and a stretch, they headed to town to find out who was making such a racket.

The dead looked in the beauty salon.
"Oh, honey, you look like death warmed over! A little dye and a trim is just what you need," the beautician said.

The dead checked in the library.

"Shhhh," the librarian whispered, "I expect dead silence in here!"

The dead searched through city hall, but all they found were skeletons in the closets.

They peeked in the post office.

"If you're looking for the dead-letter office," said the clerk, "it's in the basement."

The dead strolled through the park, where the garden-club members were hard at work.

"Surely, it wouldn't be any skin off of your noses to lend us a hand, would it?" they asked.

The dead worked their fingers to the bone pushing up daisies.

They searched the community pool, which was a boneheaded thing to do, since they were dead in the water. "Man, that's one awesome dead man's float!" exclaimed the lifeguard.

The dead had searched the entire town without finding the culprit. By the time they reached the outskirts, their feet were killing them. With bone-dry mouths, they sat at a final resting place and buttoned their lips to listen. The noise was dead ahead!

When they finally caught up with Henry, he was teaching
his dog how to roll over and play dead. Henry saw them
coming and could guess from their deadpan expressions that
they had a bone to pick with him. If his family found out the
trouble he'd caused, he knew he'd be a dead duck.

"Maybe if I'm really quiet, you can go back to sleep."
So Henry tried tiptoeing while he walked and whispering when he talked. He chewed with his mouth closed and stopped snapping his gum, but the dead couldn't go back to sleep.

He read quietly without moving his lips, but the dead were still not sleepy.

He even tried taking a nap himself, but it was no use. Even though the noise had died down, the dead were wide-awake!

Henry tried to tire them out with an energetic game of kick the bucket. Even after the sudden death overtime, they wanted to play another game.

He organized a cross-country race. They put their best foot forward, but they finished in a dead heat.

He gave a booby prize to the one who came in dead last.

He held an arm-wrestling competition. Unfortunately, the championship match ended in a deadlock.

Showing them a picture of his sister, first thing in the morning, truly scared them. It just didn't scare them to death as he'd hoped it would.

Then Henry had an idea that stopped him dead in his tracks. He'd throw a party!

You're invited to the First Annual
DEAD FOLKS SLEEP OVER
Tonight
At the graveyard
B.Y.O.B. (bring your own bones) for loads of fun.
No need to R.S.V.P. if you want to
R.I.P.

Every body came to the sleepover. They wouldn't have been caught dead anywhere else!

There was music and dancing. They rattled their bones to "Body and Soul" and shook a leg to "Stayin' Alive." They even tried break dancing to "Another One Bites the Dust!"

They had a costume contest. The winner was a dead ringer for George Washington.

Henry showed them a movie while they munched on finger sandwiches.

The Legend of Sleepy Hollow

IN REMEMBRANCE

And when it was really, really late and the moon was dead center in the sky, Henry announced, "It's time for a bedtime story!"

So the dead snuggled in their graves and their crypts and their mausoleums and they puffed up their pillows. When they were all settled in, Henry read them a really long, really sleepy story. When he got to the end, the dead whined, "Uuuggh Muuurr! Uuuggh Muuurr!"

"Okay, okay, one more time, but that's it," Henry said.

So, in a really low, really quiet voice, he read the story for a second time.

When Henry looked up, the dead were sound asleep.

Henry was dead tired himself after such a long day.
So in the dead of night, he headed home. And if you think
that Henry learned his lesson, you'd be dead right. He
was just thankful that it was . . .

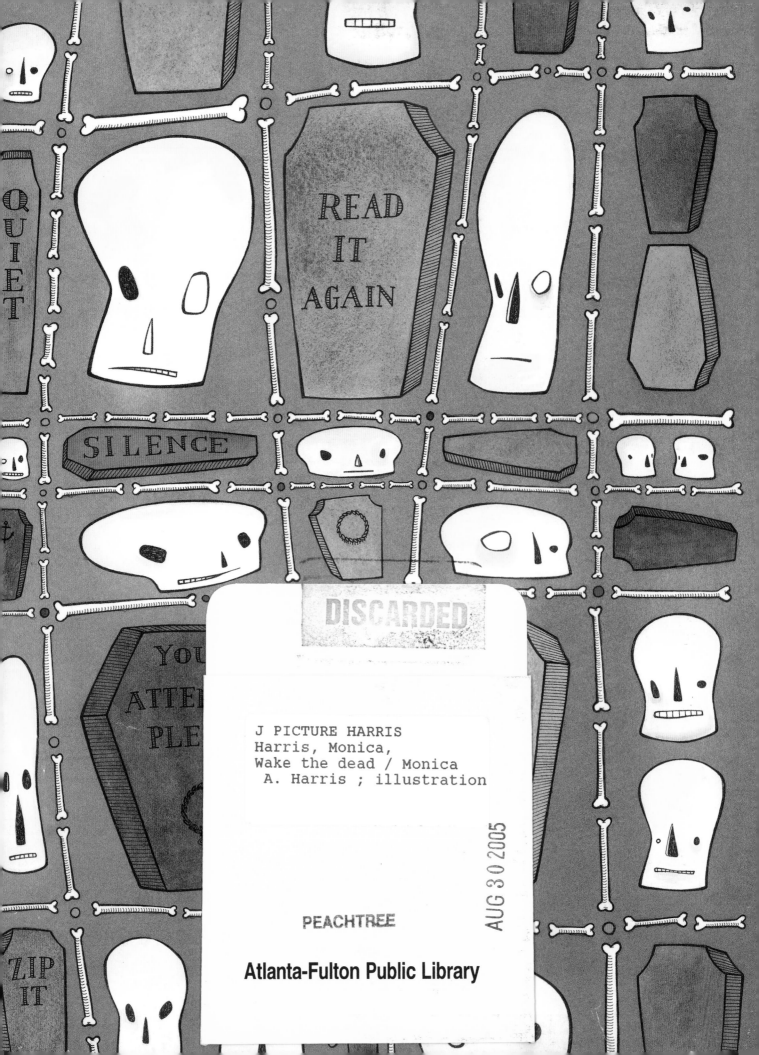